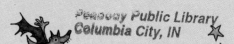

DANGER

MONSTERS ON THE PROWL!

THE BASILISK

Feared throughout ancient times. Habits recorded by the Roman author Pliny the Elder. Half serpent, half rooster. Hatched from an egg. Small but deadly! See page 6.

THE BUNYIP

A monster of Aboriginal mythology. Inhabited billabongs and other water holes of Australia. Devoured human prey. Made a booming noise. Check it out. See page 10.

GRENDEL

Swamp-dwelling monster of Norse legend. Liked devouring Danes. Had a wicked mother. Read all about him in the Anglo-Saxon epic poem BEOWULF, or turn to page 14.

THE CHIMERA

A three-headed, fire-breathing monster. The Greek poet Homer wrote about it. The people of Greece feared it. The monsters Typhon and Echidna created it. Do you dare read about it? See page 20.

ISIKUKUMANDERU

An African she-monster. Lived in rivers. Known in Bantu folklore. Very smelly and quick-tempered, not to mention greedy and deceitful. Swallowed people whole. Would steal the shirt off your back. Want to read more? Turn to page 26.

*For my
monstrously
good friend,
Wendy*

*The author and publisher gratefully
acknowledge the Brambuk Aboriginal Cultural Centre
and the Gariwerd Aboriginal Communities of the Southwest
and Wimmera region of Victoria, Australia for permission
to retell the story* The Bunyip.

First U.S. edition 1999

Williams, Marcia.
Fabulous monsters / retold and illustrated by Marcia Williams. —1st U.S. ed.
p. cm.
Summary: Five stories, told in cartoon form, about legendary monsters
including Grendel, Isikukumanderu, the basilisk, bunyip, and chimera.
ISBN 0-7636-0791-6
1. Tales 2. Monsters—Folklore. 3. Animals, Mythical—Folklore. [1. Monsters—Folklore.
2. Animals, Mythical—Folklore. 3. Folklore. 4. Cartoons and comics.] I. Title.
PZ8.1.W6545Fag 1999
398.21—dc21 98-46838

2 4 6 8 10 9 7 5 3 1

Printed in Hong Kong

This book was typeset in Stone Informal, ITC Tempus Sans Bold,
Gararond Bold, and Journal Bold.
The illustrations were done in pen and ink and watercolor.

Candlewick Press
2067 Massachusetts Avenue
Cambridge, Massachusetts 02140

FABULOUS
MONSTERS

retold and illustrated by

Marcia Williams

CANDLEWICK PRESS
CAMBRIDGE, MASSACHUSETTS

THE BASILISK

During the night of Sirius the Dog Star, on an Atlantic island, an egg was laid by an ancient rooster. The rooster buried the egg deep within a dung heap.

In time, the egg hatched and out came a BASILISK—

a small, sinister monster who could kill with a glance.

Just a whiff of its breath could burn up birds in flight.

Even the sound of its hissing could prove deadly.

Only the weasel was immune to the Basilisk's menace, and only the plant rue did not wither in its path.

With so few enemies, it did not take many Dog Star nights for the small island to become overrun by Basilisks.

Animals hid beneath the ground. Not a soul dared venture outside, not even to collect food. Hunger and fear gnawed at their bellies, but neither man nor beast could think of a way to destroy the Basilisks!

One brave knight did try. He set forth with his ears and nose blocked and his eyes hidden from the "death glance" by bunches of rue. He succeeded in spearing a Basilisk, but so potent was its venom that the poison shot up through the knight's spear, killing both him and his horse.

The islanders had resigned themselves to death, until Patrick was washed up on the island's shore. Patrick had escaped from vicious pirates by diving overboard, little realizing that he was approaching a far greater danger: the lethal Basilisk!

Luckily, brave Marie spied Patrick through a crack in her curtains.

Marie dragged Patrick inside before the Basilisks could kill him.

To show his gratitude, Patrick decided to destroy the Basilisks.

First, he asked Marie to sew him into a leather suit.

He hung sparkling mirrors all over this suit,

so that all who came near could see their reflection.

Then, after blocking his nose and hiding his eyes behind rue,

Patrick left the safety of the house.

The island was a wasteland—even the rivers ran without life. Not a creature stirred, not even a weasel. Patrick shivered with fear, and the mirrors tinkled.

Alerted by the sound, Basilisks charged from every direction. The Basilisks drooled in anticipation of a kill, but Patrick stood firm. As the first Basilisk pounced with open jaws, it caught sight of itself in the mirrors!

It dropped to the ground, dead cold! Soon Patrick was surrounded by dead Basilisks. One look in Patrick's mirrors and their own "death glance" killed them. Patrick had found a way of destroying the venomous monsters with cunning as his only weapon.

As Patrick roamed the island in his glittering suit, weasels began to come out of the ground to help him. The weasels hunted down the Basilisks and drove them to look at themselves in Patrick's mirrors, until every Basilisk on the island had been killed by its own "death glance."

Free to roam their island again, the people prepared a feast of thanks for Patrick, their savior. Patrick decided he would not risk being captured by pirates again but would stay on the island and protect his new friends. They were delighted, for they never knew when an egg might be laid by an ancient rooster on a Dog Star night!

THE BUNYIP

From the beginning of time, the monstrous, bellowing Bunyips have lived in the swamps and water holes of Australia, devouring any man, woman, or child who unwittingly strays into their territory.

One day, Tall Toby and his brother Maxi went in search of food for their family.

On an island in the middle of a billabong they found a nest of swan eggs.

Tall Toby and Maxi took half the eggs, then waded back to the bank.

By now the pair were ravenous, so they built a fire and roasted some eggs.

Soon they had eaten all the eggs!

Tall Toby forbade Maxi to fetch more eggs in case a Bunyip was watching.

Maxi thought of his hungry family and ignored Tall Toby.

Maxi splashed back through the billabong.

He found the swan's nest and took all the remaining eggs.

As Maxi returned, the water began to boil up.

All the waterfowl rose into the air.

The soft billabong mud sucked at Maxi's feet.

Maxi was very frightened. He could no longer move.

Then a great wave caught hold of Maxi.

The wave lifted Maxi back toward the swan's nest . . .

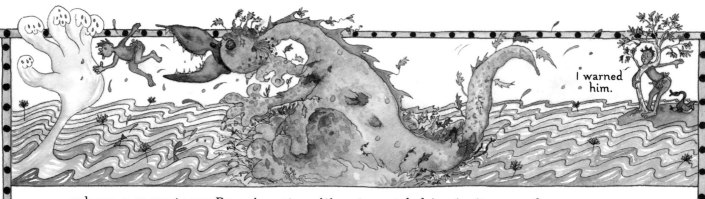

where a monstrous Bunyip sat waiting to catch him in its mouth.
Tall Toby watched from the bank and feared for Maxi's life.

So Tall Toby found a
large piece of bark,

took some sticks from the fire, and set out to rescue
his brother from the Bunyip.

Tall Toby begged the Bunyip
to spare his brother's life.

But the angry Bunyip only snarled at Tall Toby, and
shook Maxi from side to side with increasing violence.

Tall Toby grabbed his sticks of fire and
showered the Bunyip with flames.

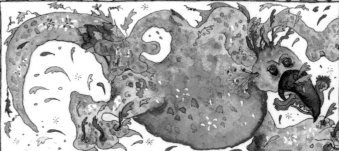

The Bunyip's hair caught fire, and
cinders burned holes in its toes.

The Bunyip opened its mouth wide and howled with pain. As it did so, Tall Toby snatched Maxi from its jaws.

Tall Toby laid Maxi on the bark and paddled quickly back to the bank. But alas, Maxi was dead.

The Bunyip, satisfied that it had avenged itself against the man who had stolen the eggs from its domain, cooled its burns in the billabong. The Bunyip was quite sure that no one would dare enter its territory again.

Tall Toby put his brother's body high in a tree for the passing of one moon.

Then Tall Toby burned Maxi's body on a pyre. Thousands of sparks lit up the night sky.

Tall Toby never returned to the billabong, but he was still able to feed his hungry family.

GRENDEL

Thousands of years ago stories were told and songs were sung about Grendel, a man-eating monster who terrorized the people of Denmark for twelve years.

The Danish King, Hrothgar, had built a magnificent hall for his warriors.

But each night, when the feasting was done and the men lay sleeping . . .

the monster Grendel arrived, savage with hunger for human flesh.

So, eventually, across the sea from southern Sweden sailed Beowulf, Prince of the Geats, with his brave warriors. Beowulf had killed many monsters and was determined to help the Danes.

As King Hrothgar dined with Beowulf and his companions, there was hope in his heart. Beowulf had the strength of thirty men in his sword arm.

After the feast all the Danes went off to their beds.

Meanwhile, Beowulf and his men secured the doors and prepared for the arrival of Grendel.

They all unsheathed their swords, except for Beowulf, who planned to meet the beast unarmed.

Suddenly they heard Grendel's terrible cry. The doors of the great hall splintered under his weight.

In a flash, Grendel had stuffed a warrior into his mouth. But before the monster could snatch another victim, Beowulf grabbed his arm and held it fast. Grendel felt an iron grip and was afraid; he struggled, but Beowulf held on. The warriors attacked with their swords, but no man-made sword could pierce Grendel's tough hide.

Then, with a tremendous effort,
Beowulf wrenched Grendel's arm
right out of the monster's shoulder.

Howling with pain, Grendel fled
into the night, leaving his arm in
Beowulf's grasp.

Beowulf and his warriors pursued Grendel across the marshy fen-land to a lake.
The bloodstained waters told them that the monster lay dead beneath its surface.

Beowulf was proclaimed a hero, and a great banquet was held in his honor.
But, as the minstrels played, a horrible roar mingled with their music.
It was Grendel's mother, seeking revenge.

That night the she-monster caught and ate a Dane.

So Beowulf and his warriors returned to the lake where Grendel had died, to seek his mother in her lair.

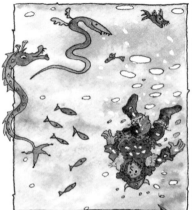

Only Beowulf was brave enough to dive into the murky water.

A great claw dragged Beowulf into a cavern. Grendel's mother attacked with ferocious strength. Beowulf's sword was powerless.

Beowulf threw the she-monster into the air.

The she-monster sat on top of Beowulf.

Then she prepared to cut Beowulf's throat.

Beowulf grabbed Grendel's sword of magic strength.

With this magic sword, which had been made by giants, Beowulf struck Grendel's mother a fatal blow.

At last the two monsters lay dead. Beowulf had freed the Danes from their reign of terror.

At the great hall, the Danes held a victory celebration and cheered Beowulf over and over again.

Then Beowulf and his men sailed home, rich with gifts and honors from the grateful Danes.

THE CHIMERA

In ancient Lycia, a she-monster called the Chimera was savaging the people of Asia Minor and laying the land to waste with her fiery breath. Many brave men had tried to destroy her, but all had failed.

Everyone was terrified of becoming the Chimera's next meal.

King Iobetes could not find anyone to defend his people against the beast.

Then Bellerophon arrived at court, ready to take on the challenge.

A soothsayer advised Bellerophon to enlist the help of the winged horse, Pegasus.

So Bellerophon prayed to the goddess Athene, as she alone had the power to catch Pegasus.

Athene admired Bellerophon's courage and gave him Pegasus's golden bridle.

Pegasus loved his freedom and was not easy to catch. But finally the golden bridle worked its magic, and Pegasus allowed Bellerophon to mount.

The two adventurers flew across the land in search of the Chimera.
Eventually, they spied the sleeping she-monster far below them.

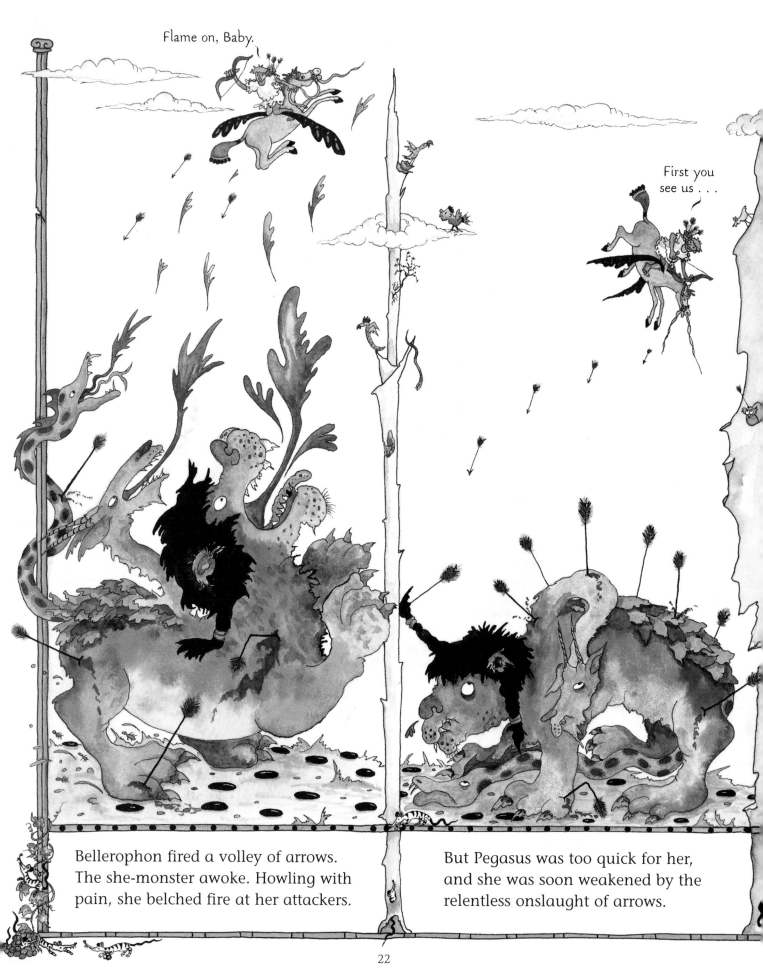

Bellerophon fired a volley of arrows. The she-monster awoke. Howling with pain, she belched fire at her attackers.

But Pegasus was too quick for her, and she was soon weakened by the relentless onslaught of arrows.

As Pegasus hovered out of the Chimera's reach, Bellerophon fixed a large lump of lead to his spearhead.

Then Pegasus dived as close to the Chimera as he dared, while Bellerophon plunged the spear deep into her throat.

The heat melted the lead and it flowed through the Chimera, searing every vital organ. Bellerophon and Pegasus watched as the she-monster was consumed by her own flames, until all that was left was a smoldering pile of ash. The brave pair had freed the people of Lycia from the Chimera's tyranny.

Yet Bellerophon felt sad, for now he must remove the golden bridle and say good-bye to his new friend, Pegasus.

But the winged horse had become fond of Bellerophon and decided to carry him in search of further adventures.

Bellerophon and Pegasus stayed together for many years. They performed numerous brave feats and won countless battles, but never again did they meet a foe as fearful as the Chimera.

Many moons ago, in the part of Africa where the Bantu people live, the great she-monster Isikukumanderu guarded the river Ilunge.

To avoid being eaten, no one swam in the river.

No one wanted to, except a girl called Ntombinde.

She bullied her father, the village chief, until he let her go.

Ntombinde went to the river with a group of friends.

The girls swam in the river until the air grew cool.

But then they found that all their clothes had disappeared.

Only monstrous footprints were left on the bank!

They begged the beast to return their belongings,

and before long she relented and threw their garments back to them.

Only Ntombinde still stood naked. She was too proud to say please.

Angered by her pride, Isikukumanderu rose up and swallowed her!

Ntombinde's terrified friends ran to the village to tell her father.

The chief sent his finest warriors to slay the monstrous Isikukumanderu.

But they were no match for the terrible beast and she ate them all up.

Furious that the chief had dared to send warriors to kill her, Isikukumanderu tore toward the village. She flattened the fence and devoured every living creature, even the chief. Then she dragged her swollen stomach homeward.

On the way she spied twin boys from a neighboring village.

In spite of being full to bursting, Isikukumanderu could not resist them!

The twins' father, Sobabli, realized their fate and set out to kill the monster.

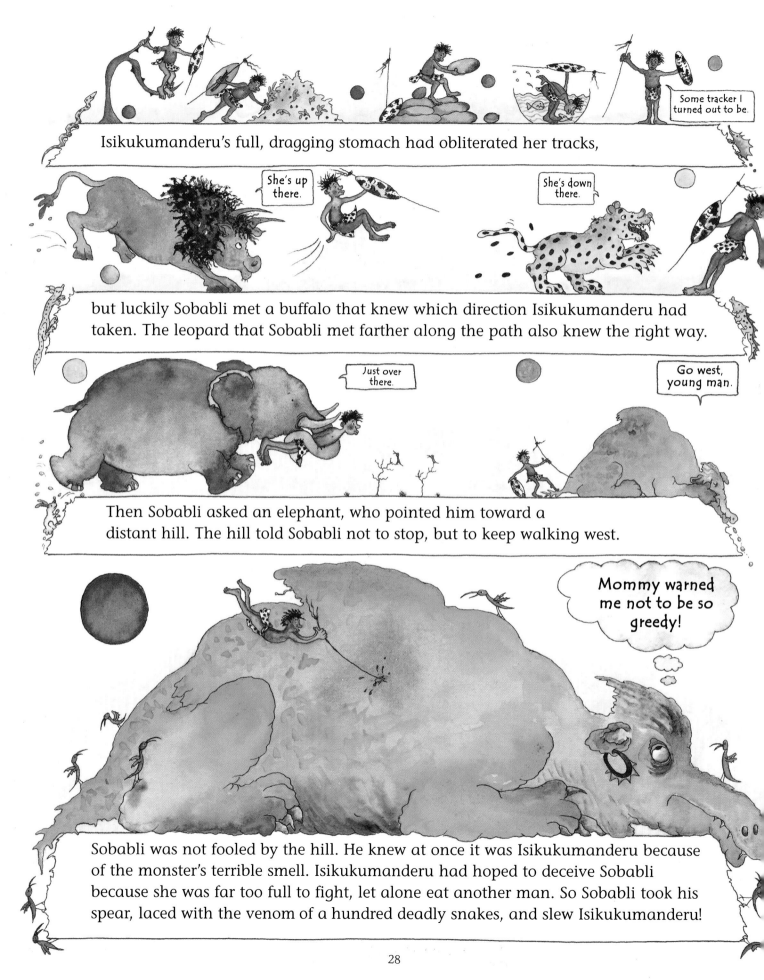

Isikukumanderu's full, dragging stomach had obliterated her tracks,

but luckily Sobabli met a buffalo that knew which direction Isikukumanderu had taken. The leopard that Sobabli met farther along the path also knew the right way.

Then Sobabli asked an elephant, who pointed him toward a distant hill. The hill told Sobabli not to stop, but to keep walking west.

Sobabli was not fooled by the hill. He knew at once it was Isikukumanderu because of the monster's terrible smell. Isikukumanderu had hoped to deceive Sobabli because she was far too full to fight, let alone eat another man. So Sobabli took his spear, laced with the venom of a hundred deadly snakes, and slew Isikukumanderu!

As Sobabli sat mourning for his twin sons, he heard a cry from inside Isikukumanderu's belly. With a shaking hand, Sobabli cut open her great hump, and out climbed every person and animal that the great beast had eaten that day, including his twin sons. Even Ntombinde was still alive, and even she managed to swallow her pride and thank Sobabli for saving them all from the great, fat, greedy monster.

The villagers made a fire around Isikukumanderu and celebrated late into the night. By morning there was nothing left of the she-monster but dying embers. Ntombinde's father scolded her most severely for her pride, and she promised to try to mend her ways. But no one ever forgot the day Ntombinde angered Isikukumanderu, and Ntombinde never gave up seeking adventures.